Peace Train

Dedicated to Greta Thunberg and all the
children of this beautiful world – C.S.

To John Lennon and Yoko Ono
and all the creative "Peace Cats" – P.H.R.

First published in hardback by HarperCollins *Children's Books*, a division of
HarperCollins*Publishers*, USA, in 2021
Published simultaneously in hardback and paperback in Great Britain by
HarperCollins *Children's Books* in 2021

1 3 5 7 9 10 8 6 4 2

ISBN: 978-0-00-847694-6

HarperCollins *Children's Books* is a division of HarperCollins*Publishers* Ltd
1 London Bridge Street, London SE1 9GF

www.harpercollins.co.uk

HarperCollins*Publishers*, 1st Floor, Watermarque Building,
Ringsend Road, Dublin 4, Ireland

Text copyright © Cat Stevens 2021
Illustrations copyright © Peter H. Reynolds 2021

Reynolds Studio assistance by Julia Young Cuffe
Hand lettering by Peter H. Reynolds
Designed by Dana Fritts

Printed and bound in Italy by Rotolito

Peace Train

written by
Cat Stevens

illustrated by
Peter H. Reynolds

HarperCollins *Children's Books*

Now, I've been happy lately,
thinking about the good things to come,
and I believe it could be
something good has begun.

Oh, I've been smiling lately, dreaming about the world as one.

And I believe it could be
Someday it's going to come.
'Cause out on the edge of darkness
there rides a PEACE Train.

COME TAKE ME HOME AGAIN.

Now, I've been smiling lately,
thinking about the GOOD THINGS to come,
and I believe it could be
something good has begun.

Oh, PEACE Train sounding louder —

glide on the Peace Train.

Come on the PEACE TRAIN.

Peace Train, holy roller.
Everyone jump up on the Peace Train!

Get your bags together,
go bring your good friends too!

Because it's getting nearer —
it soon will be with YOU.

Now, come and join the living.
It's not so far from you.
And it's getting nearer –
soon it will all be true.

Oh, Peace Train sounding louder. Glide on the Peace Train.

Come on the Peace Train.

Now, I've been crying lately,
thinking about the world as it is.

Why can't we live in BLISS?

'Cause out on the edge of darkness
there rides a Peace Train.

Oh, Peace Train, take this country

COME TAKE ME HOME AGAIN!

AUTHOR'S NOTE

Hello and peace be with you!

I'm so very happy to share the words of my song "Peace Train" with you. I wrote these lyrics more than fifty years ago, and I know the words still boom as true and loud today as they did in the 1970s. It's incredible to see how Peter Reynolds has made the words jump to visual life for a new generation with his joysome illustrations.

Each of us has the power to imagine and to dream. We all have our own picture of what a place called "heaven" would look like, and the ONE thing — for sure — we'd all expect to find there is PEACE. That's what my song is based on: a train gliding to a world we all would like to share.

The heart is where peace begins, so fill it up with as much love as you can and let it spread outward until other people can see and feel it — be like the sun in the shadows.

Jump on board the Peace Train and let's travel together.

Yusuf / Cat Stevens